CW00868271

The Forgotten

Celeste Majcher

Author: Celeste Majcher
Book cover: Annemarie Buchner
Set in Franklin Gothic Book 12pt
First Edition 2020
Copyright © Celeste Majcher
ISBN 9798655071834

All rights reserved.

No part of this publication may be reproduced, stored in a retrieval system, or transmitted in any form or by means – electronic, mechanical, photocopying, recording – without the prior written permission of the publisher or copyright owner.
Published and printed by Malherbe Publishers

Introduction

As a care worker I was tasked with looking after many vulnerable people. Some young, some old, most completely forgotten. Each and every one of them had a story to tell and most of their stories were incredibly sad but beautiful. This book is a collection of thirteen fictional stories inspired by the lives of and conversations with these people. Some stories are lived to be told. Some stories are too important to be lost. The characters in these stories are already forgotten. It would be a tragedy to forget their stories too.

The Author

Celeste Majcher is a proud South African, born and raised in the beautiful Mpumalanga province. She currently lives in Scotland with her British husband and five children. She has an honours degree in Psychology and working with people and writing have always been her two greatest passions. She worked as a care worker before her second pregnancy and fell in love with her clients and their forlorn lives. She was sad to give up her work prior to the birth of her daughter and saying goodbye to her clients was heart breaking, but she knew that she wanted to be home for her children instead. A couple of years later they were blessed with triplets and she is loving her current role as full time mum, wife, homemaker, and freelance writer.

To my amazing husband, Iain. Thank you for believing that I could do it and for pushing me to try. I will always love you.

Contents

Do You Know Loneliness?

Do you know loneliness?
Have you ever felt it creep into your very being and nestle there, long enough to make you want to die? Have you ever heard the deafening silence with just your own breathing to fill the time? Have you ever been alone for so long that you are too scared to open your front door and peer out in case someone looks in your direction and you have forgotten how to interact with people?

Let me tell you about loneliness.

In Dundee's city centre is a huge building, a beautiful building, filled with many flats. I can only tell you about the one which I had the privilege to see on the inside. It was a beautiful two-bedroom flat with huge windows, wooden floors, and a modern kitchen. On the outside, the area spoke of wealth, with modern boutiques, delis, and little cafes between all the houses. It was only when I had to ring the bell three times as proof that I was indeed a care worker and not someone with ulterior motives, that I realised not everything in this neighbourhood was as it seemed.

Once I was buzzed in, I ran up the stairs because I was already a bit late, and somewhere on one of the top floors, I heard a door creak open. With an upward glance I could only make out two pale pink slippers.

'Are you OK, dear? Can you manage the stairs?' echoed a timid and hoarse little voice.

And then I saw her. Lorna was the smallest and most frail human being I have ever laid my eyes upon. A gentle breath would have knocked her over. Her black hair was glued to her head and her pyjamas and dressing gown seemed to be sculpted onto her body. The poor woman was half blind, nearly completely deaf and rheumatism had bent her neck down ninety degrees, which meant that she was unable to lift her chin off her chest. She had to stand to the side, tilt her head slightly and close one eye to see me properly.

As soon as I crossed the threshold, the reality of it all hit me. I don't think she had seen the other side of the front door in years. As she struggled to close and lock the door to her own flat, I realised that her condition prohibited her from climbing the stairs, and that she had no strength to face the world beyond. My job was to help her have a bath, but judging by her poor state, I realised that she had not felt a drop of water on her skin for weeks, maybe even months. Before I could ask her if she wanted a bath, she told me that she didn't need one and would prefer if I would use the time to sit and talk to her instead. I tried my best to explain that I would be happy to talk to her during the bath but she refused, and I realised that as with everything else, too much time had passed since her last bath and it had now become just a little too scary to attempt.

After some discussion, we finally settled down with a coffee and I was glad to see her release the anxiety of an unwanted bath by a complete stranger with a sigh. I looked around, trying to give her some time to adjust to my presence, and I was surprised to see the number of books and newspapers stacked along the walls. The tables and chairs were stacked with even more items, some precious, most completely and utterly useless and before long I found myself analysing her hoarding tendencies. 'Tell me if you see a little cockroach, dear?' she chimed into my thoughts. Having never really loved the little critters, I lifted my feet ever so slightly off the ground and asked if she had a problem with cockroaches in her flat?

'Oh no, I don't, but the landlord does. You see, I have always been alone. I worked at the pharmacy all my life and when I was finally too old to stack the shelves, they suggested that I retired. And so I lost the biggest part of who I was. I had no family left and I had no friends to speak of. The pharmacy was my entire life. I ended up in my flat, day in and day out, all on my own.'

'Until one day, when someone rang the doorbell. He sounded so sad on the entry phone that I just had to let him in. He came in and explained that he was homeless, hungry and in desperate need of a bath. So I gave him a meal and some coffee, he had a nice long bath and I felt so much better for finally being able to help someone again. I felt a little more human again. Like I mattered, somehow. I was even a little sad when he left a few hours later.'

'That same night, around 3am, he rang the doorbell again, this time to ask if he could move in with me. The way he explained it made so much sense. He would protect me in return for a place to stay and some food.'

'I was in my late fifties at the time, and he was thirty-five. It was a good arrangement. He stayed in the spare room and ensured that all the lights were turned off and the doors were locked at night, and when things were broken, he would fix them. In return, I would cook for him and do his laundry. There were times when he was a bit violent, but he wasn't a bad man. It was just a lifetime of sadness that became a bit too heavy from time to time.'

'I think he was the only friend I ever had. The only real friend. In my forty years at the pharmacy I saw hundreds, if not thousands, of people. Most of them were friendly but there were the odd nasty ones as well; no two customers or colleagues were the same. The only constant was the knowledge that they would leave again. Some, as soon as they found what they needed. Others, in pursuit of greener pastures. It taught me not to become too attached to people and it served me well. At least until my retirement.'

'When Gerry arrived that night, I knew he wasn't going to stay for long either. I just knew it. And I was right. After about two years of conversations and camaraderie, he was diagnosed with a very aggressive cancer and he was given a few short months to live. His children and family wanted nothing to do with him, and I was the only person in the world who was willing to look after him. I vowed that I would look after him until the very end, and that is what I did.

They supplied him with a hospital bed and turned my kitchen into his bedroom. He spent the last few months of his life here. I was always by his side with food and water, a cold compress for the fever or a warm blanket for the shivers. I looked after him to the absolute best of my abilities, but death still came to take him home.'

'I didn't have any money to pay for a funeral, so the council took him away and buried him somewhere. I don't even know where. And I have been alone ever since.'

'Golly, I never even told his children of his death! Although they don't really deserve to be told. I mean, to disown your own father like that! No, I don't think they deserve to share in the details of his final few years and months on earth. Not yet anyway. I might tell them later.'

'After they finally came to collect his bed and other equipment, I was left with a very empty house. That is when I first spotted them. Two small eyes in the corner of my room. At first I felt a bit scared, but then I thought that perhaps it was Gerry who had come back in the form of this little creature, to tell me that he was OK. So I broke a piece of Gerry's favourite biscuit and can you believe it? The little insect came closer and ate it up! And then he asked me for more! That's when I knew Gerry was alive and well and I was lonely no more.'

'We had such lovely conversations. Or rather, I had lovely conversations. He was such a good listener. And what an appetite! I must have fallen asleep at some point because when I finally woke up again, I was still sitting in my chair and all the lights were on. My little critter friend had disappeared though, and I was just about to feel the sadness creep in again when I spotted him trotting into the room, this time with two of his friends! We talked some more, and I slept some more. I can't tell you if it was night or day because time was not a solid construct anymore. I just know that I felt so incredibly happy again.'

'It was only when there were a few thousand of them that I realised I would not have enough food for all of them. My pension wasn't enough to keep feeding them all, so I had to scale down a bit and make my portions slightly smaller but that did not put them off in the slightest. They kept coming back and they kept spreading the word!'

'I'm not stupid. I knew it was becoming an infestation, but it was so nice to have some life in these four walls again, that I tried to extend it just a little longer. But the neighbours phoned the landlord when the scratching on the floor became unbearable. It made sense, as there were so many that it looked as though the floor was moving with all of them. It was only when they started running up and down my curtains that I started to feel a bit scared as well.'

'The landlord was very angry with me. He shouted a lot before finally calling pest control. I knew what that meant. Those people would come and kill them! And it wasn't their fault that I started feeding them. So, when the men finally arrived, I decided not to open the door. I chose not to open it every day that week, and then they finally stopped bothering us.'

'At least, that is what I thought.'

'A few weeks later they came to get me. The ambulance and social worker. They took me to a retirement home so that they could fix my flat. It took them nearly a year. They had to redo the floors, the walls and the ceilings and they got rid of everything I owned, the furniture, pictures, books, everything. They later told me that they had to renovate the entire building.'

'When I was finally allowed back inside, there was no sign of life left anywhere. Everything was gone. All of my possessions. Everything I had of Gerry. Everything I had of my late mother and sister. I had nothing left. I haven't been able to get rid of anything since.'

'However, the absolute worst part, was that there were no cockroaches left. Not even a single one. I now spend my days staring at the floor, listening to my own breathing. I can't really see the television and the radio doesn't have good reception. Don't get me wrong, I enjoy the visits of all you lovely ladies, but it is only for an hour a day and that is not really enough.'

'So, I have started to leave a few crumbs out every night. Just a few, mind you, as I don't want to encourage them too much. Just in case they survived and need some more food. Surely you can understand that? Please don't tell my landlord.'

Loneliness is to open the door to a homeless man when you are the wrong side of fifty and allow him to stay, just to feel human again. Loneliness is to stop washing and dressing because there is no one to see you. Loneliness is to wait for that bell to ring three times a day to allow someone in for an hour's conversation. Loneliness is to hope, with every ounce of your being, for a little cockroach to reappear to eat a few of your crumbs.

The thing about loneliness is, it is so incredibly lonely.

My Existence was a Mistake

At the glorious age of ninety-five, Audrey is smaller than I could ever have imagined. I have to knock twice before she hears me and when she finally opens the door, I am greeted by a tiny little body, bent over from years of walking upright and a huge crown of white curls, testament to the fact that she has not been awake long. The calluses on her hands remind me of my own granny and I suddenly feel a protective instinct towards her. I wonder what her story might be. Where is her family? What has happened for her to live alone on the outskirts of Glasgow with only the birds for company?

'Come in! Why are you just standing there? You must be freezing there in the wind! Come in and have a nice warm coffee!' The voice accompanying these friendly, yet firm, commands is deeper and stronger than I anticipated, and I am suddenly at a loss for words. This woman is not as near death as her age implies. In fact, she has more strength and force in her tone than I have had all morning and her bright blue eyes tell me that she still has a lot to say...

I feel like a little girl again as I allow her to usher me inside while trying to pretend that I am still in control of the situation. I am supposedly here to look after her! 'Go, make yourself some coffee. I can't stand for more than a few minutes, so I won't be able to make it for you. No, none for me, I just made my own. The kettle has just boiled, the coffee powder is in the cupboard and the milk is where you'd expect it to be. And when you're done, you can come and sit with me and tell me a little about yourself. I hate it when they keep sending me new people. How am I supposed to feel comfortable with you washing me if I know nothing about you?'

With the news blaring loudly in the background, I scurry around to make my coffee whilst glancing in her direction to ensure she has something to eat. She has helped herself to a few pieces of toast with marmalade and a hot coffee and is listening to the news with only half an ear. The other is cocked in my direction to check that I am not destroying her kitchen. After a few minutes I feel more at ease and walk back to the lounge armed with a steaming coffee and the confidence I nearly left outside.

'So, tell me, who are you and where are you from? You look fairly intelligent, so what on earth made you choose to do such a simple job as care work?'

That initiated the formal introductions and I told her all about my life up until that point; how I ended up in the United Kingdom and how my life had taken a completely different direction to the one I had originally planned. She did not shy away from any of the difficult questions and after about ten minutes she knew almost all of my secrets. She had unearthed every ounce of my being; examined it, polished it, and returned it to its rightful place. My coffee was not even cold yet and my entire life was laid bare on the rug in front of her. 'Good. Now I know a little more about you. I think you are a remarkable and very strong young woman, even though you may not think so yourself. Now let me tell you a little bit about myself.'

According to Audrey, her existence was a huge mistake. Her father was a well-respected doctor who got married later in life. Both her parents enjoyed the status and lifestyle that came with his profession, but she assured me that was not the reason for their desire to remain childless. In fact, if it hadn't been for all their allergies, they might even have enjoyed bringing her into this life. No, nearly a hundred years ago their allergies were an unthinkable burden to carry and they had no intention of passing them on to any children. Her father was a true scientist and he made such a convincing case that his wife couldn't even begin to disagree with him. No, they agreed that there were to be no children.

It worked quite well, until a few years later when Mrs Doctor started to feel ill. They couldn't work out what ailed her and for months she stayed indoors, feeling faint and sick. Finally, at his wits 'end, her husband sought help from an esteemed colleague who took one glance at her before declaring with a massive smile that she was in fact 'with child'. They were appalled. It was already too late for an abortion without risking the mother's life. There was nothing to be done except carry this baby to term and then allow it to be born.

It wasn't an easy birth, she had been told, but it was nothing compared to the life she could expect for herself. They loved her dearly, but they continually told her that she was not only a surprise, but also a massive mistake, one they deeply regretted. She was likely to have inherited a host of allergies from both of them and she had to prepare herself for a lifetime of struggle just to survive.

However, after a few short years it became evident that her allergies would not be the pinnacle of her sad existence. Her mother was diagnosed with a very aggressive form of leukaemia and died within a few weeks. A few months later, or maybe it was years, it's all the same for a child, her father remarried. They were living in Italy at the time where she enjoyed a carefree and happy existence, unaware of the First World War or any dangers. Until the day when she was summoned to her father's study to be told that she would be sent to Britain by train because war was coming, and that she would be safer with her aunt. Before she knew what was happening, she was put on a train and sent on her way, just in time to miss the mass bombings and death of her dear father and stepmother. Shortly after her arrival in Britain she was told about the loss of her parents and she finally met her great aunt and sole living relative. This would be her new home and like so many other children, she had no choice in the matter.

She remembers the days of grey clothes and dark skies but even more acutely, the poverty in which they lived. As the only child of a successful doctor she was used to certain luxuries such as a large house with servants. Now, she had to make do with a one bedroom flat and an aunt who had no idea how to look after a child. There was not enough money for food and clothes and there was no chance of returning to school. She started working as a maid alongside her aunt and that is where she met the Lady. The Lady was a spinster with no living relatives, and as part of her Christian duty, she decided to take legal responsibility for little Audrey and give her the life she would not have had otherwise. She moved in with her and the Lady paid for her to go to one of the best schools in the country. This is a part of her story that she is incredibly proud of. I can see it in the way she pulls her aged shoulders more upright and the vigour with which she speaks of it all.

She spoke of a school where they invested in not only academic knowledge but also a wide range of life skills. They each had their own fruit or vegetable garden to tend, and the pickings were used at dinner each night. They were taught how to run a household, how to cater for large gatherings as well as basic accounting and language studies. 'I didn't know much love in my life, but at least my Lady gave me an education to be proud of. One that would serve me well as I grew up.'

A few years later Audrey met her husband and unlike all the stories we usually hear, this was not love at first sight. She doesn't regard herself as pretty and her husband was no Adonis either, so it took quite a few meetings to develop a love for each other's intellect instead. After a decent courtship, they finally got married and they had a very happy life, having of course discussed the condition of no children. With an upbringing like she had had, it was no surprise that she didn't want to bring another allergy-ridden baby into the world.

Since they were not to have children, she was allowed to focus on her career as a Clerk in the Forestry Commission and she was very well-known as an intelligent and hard-working lady. Her passion and drive made her a much-loved but also very strict boss, and everyone knew not to get on the wrong side of her. She giggled about the time when one of her juniors asked if she could dye her hair over the weekend. She told her that she was welcome to, as long as she secured another job for herself for Monday!

The Second World War was related with the same clinical coldness as every other part of her tale. It was just another one of those things that had to be survived. Her husband had to go away to fight and she had to keep the household running in his absence. If he died, then so be it. However, she was very glad when he came home.

She finally knew love and joy, but it was the friendship and companionship of marriage that she missed when he passed away, long before she did, not that she expected much else, of course. She used her inheritance to buy this little flat on the outskirts of the city and planned to spend the last few years of her unwanted life there.

I have to admit, with each passing word and sentence I waited. I waited to hear of the psychological damage and problems this woman had developed during her lifetime. Even just one small part of that life would be enough to drown most people in either a depression or an array of unhealthy coping mechanisms. Yet not her. Every single story, every single memory started with 'I was so lucky;' 'I was so blessed;' 'Can you believe my fortune?' 'I should not have existed, yet my parents still loved me and cared for me, regardless of how much work I must have been in my early years.' 'I am so blessed as I would have been killed in that bombing had I stayed even one day longer.' 'I was so fortunate to end up at my aunt's, because that is where I met my Lady.' 'I did not experience much love, but I am so fortunate to have received such an amazing upbringing.' The list goes on and on.

After an hour of talking we were finally ready for her bath and the styling of her hair. It all happened fairly quickly and 20 minutes later I was standing at the door and felt her small cold hand in mine as she gave it a proper shake and said: 'Goodbye my dear. You are a remarkable person and even though you are struggling at the moment, I know you will overcome this darkness. Now, head up, look the world in the eye and LIVE.'

I wonder if she would ever know how important that meeting was for me? For someone who should not have existed, meeting her became one of the crucial moments of my existence and I suspect I am not the only one to have known such fortune.

Young and Crippled

John Q's house overlooked the North Sea. It was a huge building with three floors and a small garden at the front and a little gate that opened onto the beach. Each room had an uninterrupted sea view and I found myself feeling just a tad jealous of the fact that someone had the privilege of waking up right next to the sea every day, feeling it and breathing it with each passing breath. What I wouldn't give for a house like that...

However, as I should probably know by now, the reality is never as it seems.

When I pushed open the door, the sea-breeze collided with a thick wall of old smoke. The smell of cat litter, which should have been chucked out weeks ago, mixed with the scent of years of accumulated dust, came wafting out and I immediately realised that this would not be an easy visit.

His bedroom was the first room on the right and as I entered, he grunted a 'Hello' and an: 'I've already done everything, you might as well go' in my direction. I hid my sigh of relief for not having to spend too long in this horrible filthy nest; but, following my training, I walked closer to formally introduce myself and I was shocked to see that the man in the bed was not even as old as my own father. He was lying in bed with a cigarette in one hand and the television remote control in the other and he paid me no attention. His eyes were fixed on the screen of some sports channel and he waved in my direction and repeated: 'I told you, I have already done everything, you can leave.'

I couldn't do that, especially since I was being paid for the full thirty minutes and my managers would not be pleased if I logged out of the visit after a meagre two, so I quickly glanced around to see if there was something that I could do for him. I spotted three mugs filled with old tea and sour milk and I asked him if I could wash those up before I left. 'If you must. And while you're at it, give the cat some food as well.'

I was relieved to find the kitchen in a much cleaner and tidier state. It was clear that most of his care workers spent the majority of time in this space, possibly because he was so irritable when you got too close to his personal bubble. I washed those mugs three times each, dried them carefully, fed the cat and gave her a few rubs and ear-scratches before I had to face the fact that these little tasks could not take me longer than five minutes. So, with my tail between my legs, I walked back into the room and asked if I could do anything else for him. 'Can you not hear me? I told you, I don't need your help! I have already done everything! Now, leave! And remember to lock the door on your way out!'

That was the end of my first visit to John Q. It lasted all of ten minutes and I left feeling sorry for myself for being spoken to in such an unkind manner.

A few weeks later, his name appeared on my roster again and this time I did not feel the tingle of excitement I usually do when I read the name of someone I already know. To be perfectly honest, I was a little disheartened and maybe even a little scared but I had no choice and so I set off to do my duty. This time I was a bit more prepared for the wall of smoke on the other side of the door and so I took a deep breath before forcing the heavy wooden frame open.

I was pleasantly surprised to see that John Q was not alone. There, on the only chair in the room of blue smoke, was a lady the size of a bus who was smoking with such passion that I could have sworn she had at least four cigarettes in her mouth. The lines on her face and her greasy hair were the only indications that she might be a distant relative of the man in the bed, but I knew what was expected of me and therefore I walked up to her and introduced myself formally. John Q had no idea who I was, and I realised there was no point in trying to explain that I had been there before, as his interest had already moved back to the football match on the telly. The lady introduced herself as his youngest daughter and casting an angry look in his direction, she told me to take no notice of his irritable demeanour. Instead, she invited me to the kitchen so that I could tell her a bit more about myself. And with that, she heaved herself upright and started swaying to the kitchen.

It turned out the invitation was not for my benefit at all. Without any warning she started telling me her entire history. She was one of three children but the only one who still visited their parents. Her sister was recently arrested for assaulting her lesbian lover and her brother lived somewhere far away and wanted nothing to do with them. All the responsibility, disappointments and costs of care were for her to bear alone, but what else could she do? She only had the one set of parents.

With each sentence I heard the loneliness in her voice, and I realised that she was stuck in a *cul de sac* of life with no means of escape. Her own two children were a proper handful; her partner had left her because her family was too crazy. She had dreams of becoming a social worker but without the means or dare I say the intellect to make that dream a reality, she found herself drifting between her own small flat, that of her ageing mother and the huge house of her disabled father.

Halfway through the sad story she instructed me to go and change her father's catheter bag but as I suspected, it was already done by the time I walked into the room and with an even angrier tone he told me to take the bag and leave him in peace!

Back in the kitchen she lifted her purse and asked me to give her a lift to her mother's flat. I must have hesitated, but she told me in no uncertain terms that as I had not done very much, and since I was being paid for thirty minutes, I still technically owed them fifteen minutes. She wasn't wrong and she pressed just the right number of buttons to get me to agree and so we swayed back to the room where she kissed her father on his forehead and I waved from the door and then we left.

I spent weeks wondering about those two visits. What on earth was the point? Sometimes, when you walk into a house, you KNOW that you will be able to make a difference, no matter how small, to that person, be it physical, emotional, mental or spiritual. Whatever it is, you get to go home after a shift knowing that you did something meaningful. But there, in that huge house with that angry and miserable man, it was unclear what impact any of us could have.

His name appeared on my roster again a few weeks later and this time I mentally prepared myself for the brief and possibly unnecessary visit. I told my husband and son to come with me so that we could spend the remainder of the time walking along the seafront for some fresh sea air.

On arrival I quietly entered his room, wearing a glove to pick up the dirty cups for a wash and I didn't even attempt small talk this time when suddenly, a soft voice croaked: 'What is the weather like today?' What a strange question. Especially since his bed was right next to the window and he had to simply lift his head to peer outside. 'Uhm, it is starting to get cold now' I heard myself say as briefly as possible, to not waste too much of his time. With a sigh that sounded like the deepest sadness I have ever heard, he said: 'That means the winter is almost here.'

'Can I do anything for you, sir?' I ask that tentative question again, fully expecting the same angry answer as before. 'Yes, perhaps you can sit on that chair and just talk to me for a few minutes. The only people I see nowadays are you ladies in your pink uniforms and my daughter.'

You could have knocked me over with a feather as I settled myself into the only chair, frantically grasping for whatever sports information I had stored in the back of my mind in case he wanted to talk about that. I need not have bothered, because as soon as I sat down, he started telling me his story.

John Q was a huge, strong man in the prime of his life. He had a beautiful wife and three young children. He had a very good job working as a labourer on a nearby farm and with his earnings he had saved enough money for a deposit on this massive house on the seafront of the now popular beach. He was a hard worker and good at his job and like all men, he enjoyed a pint at the local pub after his shift. He was a talented football player and had scored many goals for one of the local clubs; the jerseys are still framed on his wall.

Then one day the farmer asked him and a colleague to chop down some trees in the woods. It was a grey, rainy day and the roads were wet and muddy, but they knew the farm like the backs of their hands, so they didn't hesitate to step just that little bit harder on the accelerator. Unbeknownst to them, the tyres and shock absorbers of that particular vehicle were badly worn, and one sharp corner would prove to be their last. The car rolled a fair distance before finally coming to an upside-down halt. The driver climbed out with a scratch on his head and John Q had to be cut out with heavy machinery. He lost both his legs just below the hip and his spine had irreparable damage.

At the age of twenty-seven, with all the spirit and soul of a man in his prime, he was left completely paralysed. Life as he knew it was lost forever. He would never be able to work again. He would never be able to play football again. He would never experience the joy of carrying his children on his shoulders again.

His sadness and disappointment soon turned to depression and after a few short years his wife filed for divorce. She couldn't bear to live life with him anymore. His children followed suit, one by one, stopping almost all contact, apart from when they needed money. You see, they all knew that he had received a handsome insurance pay-out, enough to pay off his mortgage and have some left over for the rest of his life. It was all he had left, and he used it to pay for our half-hour visits each day. Care wasn't cheap, especially not from the company I worked for, but at least he got what he paid for and he had someone stopping by every day to see if he was still alive. That was more than he could say of his own flesh and blood.

With a heavy heart and tears in my eyes, I leaned over and gave his hand a long squeeze and this time he didn't reject my touch. In fact, when I tried to release my grasp, he held on, just a little tighter, for a little longer.

'You wouldn't believe me, but this was once a beautiful house. All the rooms were clean and tidy and each and every window opened up to the fresh sea-breeze. There is nothing quite like irony, is there? Here am I, privileged to own one of the largest houses on the seafront of one of the most popular beaches, and I do not have the legs to carry me out of my front door. Truth be told, I don't even have the strength to lift my head so I can enjoy the view anymore.'

As I left his house I was reminded of my jealousy before my very first visit. It is remarkable how context can change everything.

I never saw him again.

Raised to be Alone

In the centre of one of the most affluent and prestigious neighbourhoods is a row of apartments that overlook a massive old church and an even older graveyard. The front door to each building hides behind large, old oak trees, planted long before my birth, and their shadows make these buildings seem even more impressive and unwelcoming. But every now and then, the sun jumps through the gaps in the foliage and engulfs the building in the most beautiful shade of gold, in stark contrast to the silvery grey of the graveyard.

This is where I met Kate. She was a beautiful woman in her early sixties who did not seem to need any support or help from a care worker. She was still able to do everything for herself, from walking to talking to eating, and she performed each task with an air of royalty. Her voice was soft and melodious, and her accent spoke of a privileged upbringing. Kate was a true lady, in word and deed.

When the doors of the lift opened, I could see her standing behind her door, waiting for me, peering through the gap left by the safety chain. As soon as I exited the lift, she opened her door and ushered me inside, as if ashamed by my presence in her hallway. She explained that she was still in her nightdress and that she did not want her neighbours to see her. She would also prefer if they didn't know she needed a care worker and in actual fact, she didn't really need a care worker, she just hadn't got around to cancelling her care package yet.

Before I managed to shrug off my coat, she had already apologised nearly a hundred times. For years of expectations and beliefs that had nothing to do with me. I gently led her back to bed where she could make herself comfortable and get used to my presence. The windows were nearly nine-foot high and adorned with beautiful velvet curtains, still drawn. She settled herself back between the silk sheets and removed her pink housecoat before finally relaxing into the large down pillows. I prepared her breakfast and tea with hot milk and served it on a beautiful tray complete with a little cosy, and she seemed content.

In between her small bites of porridge and apple mousse she started telling me her story. A few months ago, she had fallen and sprained her knee and broken her arm. The fall was the start of a range of tests and procedures to determine why she constantly felt tired and lightheaded and I still don't really understand what they found. All I know is that it had something to do with an iron deficiency and her red blood cell count and that she needed weekly blood transfusions, chronic medication and intensive medical care for nearly half a year.

After about six months she was allowed to return home, but she realised that she would not manage without help. She could do the basics such as cook and shower, but she could not clean or iron anymore. So she contacted my employer for daily support. Now, months later, her arm and knee had healed successfully, and she should have technically been able to do these things for herself, but she hadn't cancelled the package yet. I started to wonder if perhaps she didn't really want to…

After a few weeks in this job you learn that there are two kinds of people in this world. Those that enjoy talking about other people, and those that enjoy talking about themselves. Both are born from an inherent need for love and acceptance. The need to feel part of something, to feel loved, to feel wanted. The need to feel important to someone else. Kate was no exception. She feigned an interest in me and my strange accent but we both knew that she was just looking for a link, the linchpin that could turn the telling back to her and her own story. So, I pulled a chair closer, made myself comfortable and started asking her about her life.

Kate was the only daughter of a very well-known and respected lawyer. Her mother was his intellectual equal, but she had not been allowed to pursue a career and was therefore only known as wife, mother and hostess. She couldn't say that she hated her role, but she didn't enjoy it very much either and therefore made it her mission to allow her daughter Kate all the opportunities she never had. Her daughter would never just be someone's wife or mother, she would have her own name, her own career, her own livelihood. She was sent to the finest schools followed by a degree in music and education at one of the best universities in the country. She was going to have a promising life, if not as a world-renowned musician, then as a teacher or perhaps even Head of a prestigious school. As a child she never really understood the nuances of her parents' marriage, but she enjoyed the attention and privileges of a rich child. Her mother passed away unexpectedly and although it was a sad time, they all felt a sense of relief as well.

Whatever her motives, her mother had ensured that she would never have to be dependent on a man.

A few short years later her father introduced her to a young partner in the law firm. He was a handsome man with such charm, and he won her heart in a few beats. It would not be long before they were married, and she was slightly better prepared for it than her poor mother must have been. She would indeed have her own career, something defining her other than just hostess and wife. She had an easy life, filled with the same luxuries she had been raised with, paired with the love of a handsome man. What more could she ask for?

Of course, she wanted children, but at the time it made a lot more sense not to have any. Without children they were both free to focus on their careers and the social aspects of his. It didn't matter really. He was so lovely. He always gave her the most beautiful, extravagant gifts and they had the perfect life. He would spend his days at the office, she would spend hers at the school and at night, if he didn't need to work late, they would spend the evenings listening to classical music and dream of the travelling they would do once they had retired. They looked forward to growing old together, but they enjoyed the here and the now of their companionship as well.

And then it happened. At the young age of sixty-five, he woke up one morning and had a massive stroke on the bedroom floor. The paramedics and doctors kept him alive for a few months, but it was only a shell that came home when he was finally discharged from the hospital. She cared for him diligently and with each passing day she realised that the light at the end of his tunnel would inevitably mean total darkness for herself.

After his death she was able to do everything that was expected of her. She planned the perfect funeral; she managed all the paperwork and financial matters. She sold their house and bought this beautiful apartment that overlooked the graveyard where her beloved was buried.

And so, her life ended at the same time as his. She had all the money in the world, an upbringing to do her proud and still, completely and utterly alone.

With a nostalgic smile she mused that her mother's work was all for nothing. No amount of schooling and/or opportunities could have saved her from the age-old dependence; born not out of need but out of love. Some people believe that the presence of children can lessen the impact of such a devastating loss. Kate will never know if that holds any truth.

With a final tear, I helped Kate through the shower and then waited outside to allow her the privacy to dress herself. She used a soft brush to tame her grey curls and then I fastened the heavy gold chain around her neck and my job was done.

We left the apartment at the same time. I had my coat and car keys; she had a vase filled with tulips. It was nearly lunchtime, and like every other day since his funeral, she would take some fresh flowers to his grave and spend a few hours in his absence.

The Embodiment of Laughter

Sarah Love looked exactly as you would imagine. Soft and cuddly with a face that shone with friendliness and love. She must have been born with a smile because the lines around her eyes and mouth testified to sixty-five years full of joyous life.

As I opened the front door I was welcomed by her helpless giggling in the lounge and as I entered the room, I saw the nurse struggling to get her support stockings onto her swollen feet. The poor woman really struggled with her veins and both legs and feet were so swollen that she could barely walk. I knew from experience with my other clients that there was nothing funny about those stockings. Skin swollen that tightly could burst open with the slightest touch and you have to use your knuckles to try and roll the stockings onto the legs. So, her giggling wasn't due to being tickled; in fact, she was enduring pain similar to being scalded with boiling water. The thing is, Sarah has spent her life laughing, even when she should have cried, and so her only response to this situation was what it always had been, laughter.

I was employed to clean her house and do some essential shopping so she could rest her legs as much as possible. She gestured me to the cleaning cupboard and gave me a quick list of tasks to do and then left me to it whilst the nurse finished her appointment. The combination of my age and the fact that I was fairly adept at cleaning meant that I soon finished all the tasks and therefore prepared myself for the second half of the visit which entailed a trip to the supermarket. She gave me her purse and a short list of essential items and then sent me on my way.

Again, buying coffee, cake and fruit can only take so long and I wondered why she would be paying for a two-hour time slot if the work could be done in forty-five minutes? Surely, she would know that it was a waste of her precious money.

It all became clear back at the house. As I was unpacking her shopping, I heard her heave herself upright and shuffle towards the kitchen, all the while chatting about this and that. And then she told ME to go and sit down so that she could make me a cup of coffee! 'No Sarah, you shouldn't do that! It is MY job to look after YOU!' But she would have none of it and practically pushed me towards the lounge. As I sat down, she asked if I wanted coffee or tea and before I could answer she declared that she makes the best milky coffee in the country and that she would spoil me with a cup of that. She asked a few more questions but then shouted that she couldn't hear me and that I should wait until she was finished.

A few minutes later she waddled back with a tray with two milky coffees and a plate of cake balanced in one hand while she steadied herself against the wall with the other. I jumped up and grabbed the tray from her and put it down on the small coffee table before serving her her own coffee and cake. 'No love, help yourself. I don't eat cake. It is not good for my weight and besides, I prefer salty snacks. Please have some, I don't get many visitors and it will spoil otherwise.' I could not believe that she sent me to the shops solely to buy coffee and cake for my own enjoyment!

'There, put your feet on that footstool, you must be exhausted from being on your feet all day. No, no need to thank me, it is the least I can do. Besides, I like doing nice things for other people. It helps me feel useful, you see.' I could feel the tears well up when it finally dawned on me that this lady paid for an extra hour every week, not because she needed it, but because she wanted to give her carer the opportunity to rest for a while. Out of sheer respect for her apparent lack of tears, I swallowed mine, lifted my feet onto the footstool and took a sip of the nicest coffee I have ever had. There is a franchise restaurant in South Africa that is renowned for its milky coffee, and for the first time in my five years abroad I tasted that piece of home again and it made me want to cry!

'You have a beautiful house, Sarah' I finally managed to say. 'Thank you love. Yes, we bought this house the day after our honeymoon.'

'We were so lucky! It wasn't even for sale. We just drove past it and we both fell in love with it straight away. My husband stopped the car and went and knocked on the door to ask if they would consider selling it to us. Now, I know you must be thinking that we must have had a lot of money, but nothing can be further from the truth. We had a tiny sum saved up as a deposit and we knew the absolute maximum we could afford to get a mortgage on and when my husband knocked on the door that day, the man answered with: "I will only sell it for this amount" and would you know it, it was the exact same amount! It was meant to be, I tell you. A few months later we moved into our dream house and immediately started trying for a family.'

'At least, that was the plan. After two years of struggling it turned out that I couldn't get pregnant naturally and in those days in vitro-fertilisation was not yet on the cards. You either could or you couldn't. So, I turned my attention to my house and my garden, and it was the most beautiful in the entire neighbourhood. Our neighbours frequently asked if they could use it as a setting for formal functions or photography sessions. My husband was incredibly proud of our house and of course of me, but I could tell that his heart was empty, and truth be told, so was mine!'

'We tried year after year and every month ended in bitter disappointment. Until one day, when I started to feel a little unwell. I went to the GP who confirmed that I was expecting a baby. Finally! Even though they had said I would never be able to conceive. I can't explain that joy to anyone. The pride and love I saw in my husband's eyes were enough to last me a lifetime.'

'You see, it doesn't help to sit in a corner and feel sorry for yourself, because it won't do you any good anyway. Things always work out the way they are supposed to.'

'I counted the days until the birth. I knew it was going to be a boy, I just knew it, and I decorated his room in the most gorgeous blues so that he would feel welcome as soon as he arrived. I did my best during the birth and managed his birth without any medication or pain relief. I swaddled him in the blanket I had knitted for him and kissed him on his forehead whilst promising him that I would be the best mummy in the world. And I was. From the moment he took his first breath we showered him with so much love and care that he had every opportunity to develop his own personality, knowing we would always support him, no matter what. He had a good childhood. I know it because he tells me every time he phones.'

'Two years later I became pregnant again. This time, without actively trying and again, I knew it would be a wee boy. The same amount of joy, pride, anticipation and love welcomed him into the world and followed him as he grew. They were our pride and joy. Just like our house and garden, our neighbours used to pride themselves on the two handsome and polite lads that came from their neighbourhood.'

'My husband died a few years later but I wasn't too sad, because we had a full and beautiful life. He was a good worker, well-known in the city and a man of stature in society with a wife and two sons to be proud of. Truly, I had a beautiful life.'

'And today? Where are your sons today?' I asked gently.

'Oh, one lives in the south of England. He has a brilliant job and a beautiful wife and three children. He is absolutely flourishing. Just like I knew he would that very first day I held him. He is a true wonder of a man.'

The younger one, lives in Canada. He still hasn't married but he is in a committed relationship and he too has a wonderful job. He won't return to Britain any time soon but that is understandable. His life is there. And from what I hear he is a real pillar in his own community. Again, exactly what I hoped his life would be.'

'They phone me every month to ensure that the house is still standing and that I still have enough money in the bank and they occasionally mention the possibility of a visit, but I don't hold out much hope. Their lives are full, and their responsibilities are many and that is fine with me. They know I love them and that they will always have a home here.'

'My husband left me enough money to look after this house and pay for your weekly visits and that is enough for me. Like I said, I had a very happy life. I am content with what I have left.'

Sarah Love looks incredibly happy with her current existence. Just as happy as I am sure she must have looked all her life. And I can't help but stare. Because from where I am standing, her smile looks sadder than a world's worth of tears.

A Shameful Heritage

The little German lady was not at all what I was expecting. When I saw her name on my roster for the first time I wondered if she was German by birth or by marriage. Her age places her birth right after the First World War which meant that she would have been in her early twenties at the start of the second. The war that changed life as we know it. And I couldn't help but wonder which side of the conflict she was on. I wondered if that was why she now lived in the United Kingdom? Had she lost loved ones in the war? Was it her choice to relocate? I wondered what her story might be.

I entered her house with all these questions still mulling around in my head and I left with a deeper knowledge and understanding than I ever expected. Some stories might take years to live, but when the time is right, a story only takes an hour to tell.

Let me tell you about Mrs Schneider-Smith.

Upon arrival I was astonished by the beauty and opulence of her house. The old cuckoo- clock outside her front door should have been enough of a clue. There was also a copper rack to clean my shoes and a solid brass umbrella stand. Once inside, my eyes were pulled in the direction of the lounge where the sun was darting through the large oak framed window and dancing on the velvet settees. In the centre of the room was a beautiful old ivory coffee table and in one corner I saw a large cabinet, filled with Eastern artefacts such as fans and hair clips, all made from solid gold. There was a magnificent old grand piano in front of the bay window and a Persian rug on the floor.

The next room had a dining table and chairs for twelve, all made from dark wood with golden trimmings. The rugs were still rich and full and by no means indicative of the age of their inhabitant.

I have been to enough castles and palaces to recognise such wealth, but never before had I seen it in a private house. And that was just two of the rooms. The bedrooms all contained beautiful four poster beds, large dressing tables and comfortable fabric armchairs.

I wondered who exactly this lady was and whether I would need to bow when I met her, when I heard her hoarse voice calling me to the kitchen.

With my heart beating rapidly I walked towards the kitchen, trying to decide how to greet her, and then I saw her. With a body smaller than that of a young teen and with hair as thin and grey as the last few feathers of an old pigeon, she sat there at the kitchen table dressed in one of her best outfits. She was wearing a beautiful long navy skirt, white silk blouse, navy pumps and a string of pearls around her neck. Each finger was adorned with a diamond ring and her eyes had the remnants of a day's make-up still clinging to her lids.

'Good evening. Is that a South African accent I hear' she greeted me, and I realised that her age may have trampled her body, but it had definitely not reached her intellect yet. 'I am Mrs Schneider-Smith and I think you are here to help me get into bed.'

Although her voice was hoarse, she managed to speak with the force and the pride of aristocracy and again I wondered what her story would turn out to be. Without waiting for an answer, she jumped up from the table, pushed her plate and glass in my direction as if to say that I should give them a quick wash, and marched off to the bathroom.

I was trained to recognise when people could still do things for themselves, and to allow that to happen rather than steal the last of their independence, and so I let her be when she closed the bathroom door with a click. I stood right outside, in the hallway, should she have needed me, but chose not to intrude on her privacy.

Ten minutes later she was finished and walked towards her bedroom. There, she sat down on the bed like a lady and held out her arms for me to take off her jewellery. Thank goodness for all the episodes of Downton Abbey I had been watching, or I would not have understood what she wanted! 'You can just put it there on the dressing table' she answered my unspoken question. Next, she lifted her hair for me to loosen her necklace and then she lifted her arms so I could take off her blouse. In those few seconds we shared more personal space and physical closeness than I have ever shared with my closest friends, but her elegance made it anything but uncomfortable.

'I once shared a meal with Nelson Mandela. He was a lovely man. A good man. Yes, it was a good experience. But wait, let me tell you the whole story.' And so it began.

'I was German by birth, and that turned out to be quite problematic. The first few years of my life were fine, but when that silly man started his nonsense, my country took a wrong turn. My parents were both labourers on a farm, with no real schooling to speak of and they lived life by only one truth, to never disagree with those in charge. We lived in the countryside, far from any of the larger cities, and we did not have much contact with the outside world. So, by the time the news about some of the atrocities arrived at our house, my parents were too scared and too helpless to fight against it. You have to remember, the news that was shared was not very accurate or factual, so it took a long time for us to realise just how bad things really were.'

'My parents worked so hard to allow me to go to school and even though the propaganda was intense, my inherent sense of right and wrong meant I could not live by those new standards. I could feel that what was happening was not right or good and I tried my best to explain that to my parents. But they were from another era and even though they agreed that it was not right, they could not imagine opposing it either.'

'Shortly before the situation in the concentration camps became known, I relocated to England, via a few other European countries. I knew it would be an all or nothing move. I knew that I would be expected to give up my heritage and pledge my allegiance to the king of this new country. It also meant that I would never be allowed to return home or see my family again. It was a sad choice but the right one. I did not want to identify as a German anymore and I couldn't think of a better way to show where my loyalties lay.'

'It was easy to find a job. My knowledge of the German language was a bonus for every news agency and I soon became well-known, not only for my work but also for my political ideas and beliefs. I met my husband at a social gathering. He was a lovely British man in the diplomatic service who was quickly climbing the ladder of success. We shared a love for each other and a hate for my country of origin and before too long, we got married.'

'A few years later, Mr Smith was chosen as the British Ambassador to a country in the South of Europe, and we couldn't wait to use our knowledge of politics and change to make a new life for ourselves. The move itself was not hard. We always had other people packing and unpacking for us, and we loved learning about new cultures and people. It was a good life.'

'We moved a few times. Each time to a different country with a different political system, each trying to find a new and better way to shape their human rights after the atrocities of that war. That meant that we played a part in the shaping of new political systems wherever we went. What a privilege for a freedom fighter like me!'

'I never saw my parents again. Our correspondence stopped somewhere in the first four years and all I know is that my dad was forced to join the armed forces and that he never made it home again. My mother stopped existing between then and now, but I will never know the details of the rest of her life.'

'It was a huge price to pay, but it was worth it for my conscience and happiness. I could not live with such atrocities then and I couldn't now.'

'But yes, let me tell you about Nelson Mandela. For years we followed the political system in South Africa, and we were very vocal about our lack of support for the Apartheid movement, so it came as no surprise that my husband was shortlisted as the ambassador for the new South Africa. He wasn't successful but we were still invited to a banquet with the first ever black president of South Africa.'

'For weeks I wondered what kind of person he would be. Other women spent their time wondering about their hair and make-up and dresses; I spent mine thinking about possible conversations I might have with the man who made reconciliation history.'

'Everyone spoke of his humility and goodness. His wise yet gentle demeanour. It was all true. But somehow, being prepared for it meant that I wasn't as surprised about it as everyone else was. What caught me off guard was his deep understanding.'

'It was finally my turn to meet him and as always, I used the opportunity to explain my heritage and my hate for it and he listened patiently.'

'It was only during the last course that he whispered in my direction: "We have a lot in common, you and I. We both spent our lives fighting for democracy and justice and we both gave up so much in the process. But all the good we achieved could never really erase who we truly are. I am and always will be the man who planted a bomb and you are and always will be the only daughter of German parents who wouldn't oppose the system.'

With a sad smile she told me that it was one of the highlights of her life, and then indicated that I had used enough lotion on her feet. With one swift movement she lifted her feet into bed, pulled up her covers and told me to shut the door quietly when I left.

Some stories are lived to be told. And just like that, without drama or ostentation, it became one of the highlights of my life as well.

Flirty but Sweet

My appointments weren't all sad. Some were funny, some were a bit strange and every now and then, even a bit awkward. Like the man who liked to surprise his carers by waiting for them in his birthday suit! Or the man who asked us on dates with a slobbery kiss on the hand.

Mr Alders was one of those.

Many of my clients were nearing a hundred, but Mr Alders was one of the only ones who had passed his first century. At the ripe old age of 105 years, I expected nothing more than a small, wobbly old skeleton either in bed or in a wheelchair, with round the clock care to keep him alive. It was therefore quite surprising to read in the notes that I should ensure he uses his cane, but I presumed that was old information that hadn't been updated recently and thought nothing more of it.

I rang the bell only once, even though I expected multiple attempts to get his attention; but lo and behold, there in the corridor I saw an alert and almost cocky man walking towards me! Surely that couldn't be him? He must have a son who lives with him, I thought. Once he opened the door, I could see the deep embedded lines in his face and a lifetime of experience in his eyes and I instantly felt as though I knew him. It is strange how your mind can trick you though. I could see how well he managed on his own, yet the knowledge of his age made me want to help him stay upright and walk and so I stretched out my hand to support him. I am not sure who was more surprised by my action, but before I could retract my hand, he grabbed it in both his hands and gave it a slobbery kiss! After that, he tucked my arm neatly over his and walked me to the lounge like a proper gentleman. There he waited until I was seated before he settled down himself.

And then the questions started. 'Where are you from, my darling? How old are you? Are you married?' 'No, I will need to speak to your husband! It is not safe to let such a beautiful woman go to strangers' houses like this.' 'Do you have children?' 'Only one? No, you need to change that. Those hips were made to bear children. You'd be able to carry at least another three or four without too much trouble!' (Are you blushing yet? Trust me, I did.) Never in my life has a stranger had so much to say about my childbearing capabilities. I felt a bit flustered and to save myself from further embarrassment, I offered to make him some coffee. Unbeknownst to him, and me at that stage, I was going to have another baby and then triplets! His prediction was spot-on!

I made it into the kitchen on my own but before I had managed to fill the kettle, I could hear him charging in behind me to help me with the cups. He told me exactly what he was cooking for supper while

I made the coffee and in next to no time, we were back in the lounge for a longer conversation.

That is how his story started.

Mr Alders hailed from one of the exotic islands in the Caribbean which was claimed as a result of British Colonisation. When the First World War broke out, he was just old enough and strong enough and therefore had no choice but to join the Armed Forces. So, at the age of 16 or 17 (he can't remember exactly), he kissed his mother goodbye, stroked her tears from her cheeks and knew that he would never see her again. It was a bittersweet goodbye, because they both knew that a better life awaited him on the other side of the vast blue ocean. And then he left.

Due to his age he first had to spend a few years as a kitchen porter, but before too long he was called to action as well. It was a really difficult war, but in all truth it was nothing in comparison to the second. That was hell on an entirely different level.

'But enough of that. You are too beautiful to be plagued by such horrible memories!' he chuckled, flushing my cheeks with yet a deeper shade of crimson.

After the war he was allowed to choose whether he wanted to return home or stay in Britain and considering that he had earned his right to stay with more blood than sweat, his application for citizenship was approved immediately. He had no schooling and no work experience, but he knew that citizenship in this amazing country would mean a better life, even for someone as uneducated as he was.

He found a job as a woodcutter in the nearby woods. He was well-known as one of the strongest men and that he could chop down many a tree on his own. (This is his tale, not mine, remember.)

Not long after he started this job, he met his lovely wife. She was a beautiful white lady who preferred a strong, dark man to all the slight pencil pushers she had grown up with. He had always had a soft spot for a beautiful woman, so it didn't take him long to ask her to marry him and start their family. She had good hips and her pregnancies were easy and beautiful. 'There really is nothing more beautiful than a pregnant woman. I can imagine you also carry your pregnancies quite beautifully.' (Cue another blushing spell.)

They had five beautiful children, three daughters and two sons. But they were a bit too greedy and wanted yet another child and so it happened, the way all things happen when you get too greedy for your own good, that both his wife and last little son died during that final birth.

It was incredibly hard and sad, but he didn't have a lot of time to sit and mope around. He had five mouths to feed and at least two babes still in nappies, so he just had to get on with it. It was still miles better than any life he would have had on the island. He didn't have any family or many friends, but he had work and he could earn a living and raise his children and that was good enough.

He was asked to retire early, at the age of fifty, as working in the woods wasn't safe for someone over fifty. He understood the reasoning but his children still needed to go to university so he couldn't just sit around at home and do nothing. He continued applying for jobs all around the city until the Head at the local school employed him as a night-time janitor. After a few years, the Head was so impressed with his work ethic that he recommended him to the community centre where he was employed in the same capacity during the daytime. It meant another fifteen years of honest work and he was so incredibly grateful for the opportunity.

He fell silent for a few minutes and then said: 'Yes, this country was really good to me. It gave me such a good life and so many opportunities. I was allowed to show my worth during the war, and can you believe it, they paid me for my duty. I got a decent job as a woodcutter and I had a beautiful wife and five beautiful children. Another two great jobs and the ability to raise my children and provide them with an education. And when I retired, I had enough money to buy this little unit in this retirement complex. The most wonderful of all is the fact that the Queen sent me a birthday card on my 100th birthday. Can you believe that?'

'Where are my children now? Two live in the South of England. One in Australia and two in America. They have, just like me all those years ago, kissed me on the cheek and waved me goodbye in pursuit of a better life somewhere else and I want that for them. Of course I miss them, but I want them to be happy. I had a good life. An honourable life. A life of abundance. And who knows, I'm not dead yet. As long as I have blood in my veins, I can still enjoy the company of a beautiful woman like you.'

With that final wink and kiss on my cheek I jumped up, washed our cups and bade him farewell.

What an incredibly lovely, albeit slightly handsy, old man. If only I could be so grateful for such a hard and thankless life. If only.

Alone with no Absolution

Elsie B's children had forgotten all about her. There isn't much else to say on the matter. The poor seventy-year old lady spends day in, and day out staring out over the back wall of her garden and there is no-one to check in, no-one to even phone to see if she is still OK. Her proud jaw and straight shoulders hide the sad softness in her grey eyes and her grey curls crown her face like a million tiny roses.

The appointments at her house are brief and easy. I knock on the door, peer into the lounge to see if she is still alive, walk to the kitchen to wash her dishes and take some milk from the freezer, ask if she wants any more coffee and then gently close the door behind me when I leave.

I always wonder why she prefers to sit in the lounge at the back of the house where she stares at the wall of the back garden, instead of the lounge overlooking the beautiful North Sea, but I never have enough time to wonder about it for too long, let alone ask. And then the appointment is over and by the time I reach my car I have forgotten about her and her house.

A week later I knock again and repeat the routine down to the finest detail, minus the coffee.

Another three visits later I remember my question and as I approach her with her coffee I wonder if it would be wise to ask. Perhaps the reason isn't one to share. 'Sit, child.' Her voice is so soft yet so clear, it forces me into obedience.

I sat down on one of the musty chairs and wondered what could be bothering her today.

'Have you seen my other lounge? The one with the sea-view? Go and have a look.'

'I have such beautiful memories in that room. That is where my husband and I kissed each other when we decided to buy the house. That is where we sat when we discussed whether to start a family.'

'We admired our firstborn, a boy, in that room. We brought in a huge spruce tree for Christmas and we loved watching our son toddle after the little steam train.'

'The following Easter it was in that very room that we told him he was going to be a big brother and by the following Christmas we were joined by our little rosebud. Years of happiness, all in that one room.'

'That is where John told us about his engagement. Where we spent evenings listening to all the wedding plans. Mary's wedding was even more of a do, all planned and discussed in that very room. Both our children knew that no matter what happened, they would always be welcome in this house where we would settle on the settee with a coffee and discuss all their problems. We would always try to give advice when we could and when we couldn't, we would all just enjoy staring out over the vast blue expanse until we all felt ready to try again.'

'When the doctor knocked on the door that day, I knew something was wrong. They don't do house calls anymore. But on that day, he did. And as was our custom, we took him to that lounge for a coffee and to discuss whatever he came to talk about.'

'He took a deep breath, looked us squarely in the eye and said: "Mr B, you are dying. Your body is completely riddled with a very aggressive cancer. It was dormant at first, which is why it took so long to diagnose but it has now spread so much that there really is nothing anyone can do."'

'I was so flustered. I hadn't even known that he had been to the doctor. And the more I asked what this and that meant, the quieter my James became. He just moved his gaze from the doctor to the sea and kept staring out over the abyss.'

'"How long does he have left?"

I asked. Two, maybe three weeks, I was told. And then he warned that they would be incredibly difficult weeks. His pain level would become/increase exponentially (higher) with each passing day and as there really was nothing more to be done, the doctor prescribed some morphine for him to use as he saw fit. It could cause severe difficulty in breathing but at that point it didn't really matter anymore. It was just a question of keeping James as comfortable as possible. He took what looked like a 4 pint bottle of morphine out of his bag and placed it on our coffee table and then walked out and closed the door quietly behind him.'-

'"James, what is going on? Since when have you suspected something? How are we going to survive this?" I had to ask each of these questions what felt like a thousand times, but he never answered. He just sat there, staring out over the sea. He was never a man to show his emotions, and so there we sat, me crying my heart out and him, silent and still, staring out over the sea.'

'Hours passed. Perhaps even days. And then he finally turned to me and looked me in the eye and said that he didn't want the children to know. I couldn't believe it. How could we possibly keep something so serious from our dear children and their spouses? They deserved to know. He is their father and they needed to know that the time they had with him was precious and oh so short. But he refused.'

'As if on cue, the phone rang at that exact moment and it was John who just wanted to see how we were. James answered and I could almost hear myself gasp in shock when he pretended that nothing was wrong. "How are Sophie and the children? Yes, we are both fine and well. Has the new kitchen been installed? Are you still planning to go on holiday next week? Yes, we are very much looking forward to seeing you on your way back. Yes of course the room is ready, and we can't wait to see you all." It carried on and on.'

'After saying goodbye, he must have seen the shock in my eyes as he pulled me closer and whispered: "My Darling, I have been doing it for years.

I have known for years that there was something wrong. But they could never find out what it was and what was the point of talking about it? I had the amazing privilege of enjoying every single one of my days because I knew that my time was precious and you, you were saved the sadness and sorrow of the wait."'

'I was so incredibly angry with him. But also so intensely grateful. The first time he noticed something was wrong was around the time of John's wedding. And there was no way I would have been able to enjoy it if I had known, not to mention John and Sophie. And later, just as Mary left for college, he had another setback, but at the time he knew that I was struggling to deal with the empty nest and wanted to save me the sadness and worry. The final bout started about 8 months ago, when Mary told us that she was expecting her first baby. And again, I could understand why he decided to keep it to himself.'

'And I finally understood why he wanted to keep it from the children as well. Mary was in her final few weeks of the pregnancy and she did not need that kind of stress and John and Sophie had only just bought a house and could therefore not afford to visit more than once during the next few weeks, and he knew that they would want to. So, the choice was made. We kept it quiet and pretended as if all was as it should be, to protect them.'

'James held Mary's little boy in that lounge and he gave John, Sophie and their two children a long hug goodbye, in that same lounge.'

'The last few days were agony. He never complained. But I could see how much he needed the morphine and I could only imagine the pain he must have been in.'

'One night, as we stared out over the sea, he held me close and thanked me with tears in his eyes for helping him protect his children from sorrow this one last time. And then he kissed me on my forehead, and I rested my head on his shoulder. And then he breathed his final breath. I sat there all night. Just like that. With my head on his dead shoulder. Crying the tears of a lifetime of memories, with the age-old echo of the sea in the background. At sunrise I got up, called the funeral home, watched as they took him away and closed the lounge door behind me as they left.'

'I knew then, just as I do now, that his final 'act of protection' would cost me everything. And it did. Once the kids found out that we had known that I had known, and chose to withhold it from them, they wanted nothing more to do with me. They accused me of being selfish. Of being a control freak. Who knows what else? It has been ten years and I have not spoken to either of them since.'

'Sophie sends me news and photos every three months and Mary's husband pays for my care package. They are building the bridge that John and Mary tore down all those years ago. They understand. Just like I had to help my James, they are now helping their precious partners, my children, by paving a way for the reconciliation they don't want to approach just yet.'

'God is faithful. I was faithful to my husband and I know God will look after me. They will come back to me again one day. They will. Because that is how we raised them. They just need to process their own grief first. And when they come back, we will open that lounge door again, open the windows to the sea and settle down on the settee with a nice cup of coffee and we will once again enjoy the lifetime of memories floating around in that room.'

'Until then I prefer to sit here. The sea lounge is a family room. And without my family, I have no right to be there.'

I would like to tell you that I comforted her with consoling words. That I held her and helped her dry her tears. But I won't. Because her story is beautiful enough, sad enough, without any more words.

I closed the front door quietly behind me, jumped down the steps two-by-two and started praying with her for a reconciliation with her children. And since then I made it a habit to ask to see the pictures of her children and grandchildren during every visit, more so than with any other client. Because her story is important. It is after all, all that she has left.

She is still waiting.

The Embodiment of Love

Bella Hope had three children. Her husband worked for the postal service and she was a stay-at-home mum, so they were never very wealthy. Her parents passed away when she was still fairly young but even then, her focus was, as it should be, on her husband and children. She was their rock, their pillar of strength and their heart.

She was a strong woman who loved her family with the same passion you see in the films in the 1950s. She raised her children with love. She was strict when it was necessary, consistent and always loving. Her children never ever doubted her unconditional love for them, and her husband was always very proud of her. She was well-read, well-dressed and intelligent enough to handle herself in any situation and the love that shone from her eyes made her incredibly beautiful. She almost never had food ready by the time he got home as she was always busy with the children, either helping them with homework or teaching them to dance, but he never cared. Their favourite memories include the times when he would get home to a house of laughter, music and dancing. He would immediately discard his coat, grab Bella in his arms and show the youngsters how to do it.

Of course, there were also sad times. Times when she missed her parents. Times when her children were trying to find their own identities by rebelling and pushing against the boundaries. But remarkably, even on those days, Bella remained the epitome of love. Don't think she was perfect. She had temper explosions, just like the rest of us, and at times her response was all but calm or tempered but her words and actions always started and ended with love. Just love. Nothing more. Nothing less.

Bella and her husband agreed that although attending a good school had immense value, it was more important for their children to have a good upbringing, something that could only be achieved by raising them at home. So they never invested too much money in the right schools or the right activities. Instead, they invested whatever money they had in their children. They were of course in a good state school, and they always had enough food and clothes and even some pocket money, but more importantly, they got weekends with both their parents. While friends bragged about possessions, they bragged about their family trips and family holidays, never too far or too expensive, but always balm for the soul. At times, their holidays were cultural, at times they focused on learning a new sport such as skiing, but that was never the main aim of these trips. The focus was always on togetherness as a family. And they achieved that remarkably well.

Bella's husband died at the ripe old age of eighty-five. They had a lovely life both before and after his retirement. Her two daughters still live in the same city as she does and although her son lives more than an hour's drive away, she still sees him more than most people see their neighbours.

At the age of eighty-seven, Bella had two massive strokes which impaired her speech, hearing and ability to move. She now spends her days in a wheelchair, unable to hear very well and even less able to speak. There are always two carers sent to someone in a wheelchair as it takes two to safely lift and move someone who is as immobile as Bella. She gets four visits a day, mainly to help her in and out of bed, feed her at mealtimes and help her to the toilet. She can't dance anymore, and she can barely sing. She can't even really talk to her family and friends anymore. But I have never been so jealous of someone in my entire life.

Not a day goes by that she doesn't get at least one visitor. Her children practically live there. Her grandchildren come to sing for and with her. One of her daughters takes her to a dance class for people in wheelchairs. Her neighbour comes to put curlers in her hair every morning. Her other daughter takes her to a nail technician once a week. And her son pays for all of her clothes. One of her neighbours looks after her garden and her children have rearranged her house in such a way that her lounge now overlooks the back garden where she gets the most sun and an almost uninterrupted view of the beautiful plants around her. All her neighbours keep an eye out for her and they are known to show up long before the ambulance or fire brigade whenever an alarm is sounded. In a country where people often don't even know their closest neighbours anymore, it is a true wonder to experience.

She has grandchildren who live as far away as Australia, but they phone her every day. She can't hear a word they say and they can't understand anything she tries to say, but they still phone, every day. And when we walk into her house her eyes light up with news of her children and grandchildren and we spend a good deal of time trying to understand what she wants to share. She was the first to be told of every pregnancy; she was present at every wedding, graduation ceremony and birthday celebration.

Bella Hope is loved. Because she is made of love. I believe that each and every person in her life is present because she first loved them. Even after the stroke that stripped her of almost everything that made her human, she is still one of the loveliest humans you would ever meet. Without a spoken word or movement of any kind, you know as soon as you walk through her door, that you are important to her. In fact, she gives herself and all her attention to you so completely that you feel like the most important person in that moment. I have read about people like that, but I have never before had the privilege of knowing one. You could honestly walk into her house at any point, night or day, and she would still look at you with such love that you know you are cared for.

Both my own grannies died just before and after my wedding and I couldn't really share much of my married life with either of them. But with every tooth that I got to brush for Bella, every sock that I got to slip on, every tiny act of service, I could show her the love that was meant for my own grannies. She could sense whenever I had had an argument with my husband or when my two-year old had a tough day and she always supported me and encouraged me, especially on those days. I still can't tell you how, as I have no idea, I just knew that she SAW me and understood.

She was one of the first clients that I told of my second pregnancy. She was so incredibly happy for me and she used her one good arm to grab me around my neck and pull me close so she could kiss me on my cheek. My growing belly was a warning of the imminent goodbye, because she knew that I would not come back, long before I knew it myself. She knew that this pregnancy and the birth of this baby would change everything for the better. It would mean the end of my depression and open my heart for a life of love, maybe even a little similar to hers.

The goodbye was incredibly hard and sad. But I walked away feeling completely at peace about her. Because I knew that she had a lifetime of hands ready to lift her and hold her whenever she needed help. The loss was a lot greater for me than it was for her.

Occasionally, when I drive through the streets of Glasgow, I imagine that I can still hear the singing. The voices of two carers and one old lady who joyfully sings: 'Daisy, Daisy, give me your answer do. I'm half crazy, all for the love of you. It won't be a stylish marriage, 'cos I can't afford a carriage. But you'll look sweet upon the seat of a bicycle made for two.' Followed by a giggle that sounds to the heavens.

I will never see her again. But I will never forget her either.

The Sadness of Two Tales

Sometimes a story belongs to two people. Perhaps because it was too heavy a burden for just one to carry. Or perhaps because that one wouldn't carry it quite right. Or perhaps it was never meant to be a burden at all.

Susan's story is one of those.

They lived fairly ordinary lives. They were somewhere on the average to upper middle-class spectrum which meant that they never had too much or too little. They always had just enough. They were involved in their community, but they were never leaders or pioneers. In fact they could probably be classed as opinion-followers instead.

They had two sons, and although they loved them dearly, there was nothing extraordinary or special about them. They were just ordinary people with ordinary lives.

Sometime after Iain's retirement, Susan was diagnosed with a tumour in her leg, and they treated it as they did everything else in their lives, with mediocre interest and an average understanding. They never expected a miracle, but they also never expected the alternative. This would not kill her, they knew that much, but they suspected that she would never truly be rid of it either.

And then on that one summer's day, they met with her surgeon and their lives changed forever. He suggested an entirely different option, one they had never even dreamed of. He was confident that he would be able to remove the entire tumour and that she wouldn't have a recurrence of this dreaded disease. With his confident assurance calming their fears, they immediately agreed to take the chance. Who were they to go against such a learned man anyway?

He made it sound like such a quick and easy procedure that they chose not to tell their boys about it at all. The operation had been scheduled for the following Friday, and on their way out the receptionist offered them some reading material about the possible risks of the suggested procedure, which they promptly declined. Why would they worry themselves for nothing? The surgeon clearly knew what he was doing.

Friday finally arrived and Iain greeted Susan with a kiss on her forehead before marching out of the hospital to do some grocery shopping. The surgeon had told him that she would be able to go home in a week's time and he had no intention of her coming back to a messy house with no food. Besides, there was no point hanging around the hospital, was there? A few hours later, according to the timeframe that was given, he walked back to her room to see her. But she was nowhere to be found. She wasn't in her room and she wasn't in recovery either. After a few hasty telephone calls between departments, they finally told him that she was still in surgery. The surgeon came out a few seconds later to update him on the fact that things had gone horribly, horribly wrong. Susan was now fighting for her life and there was no guarantee that she would make it. There wasn't much time to explain what had happened, and as the surgeon rushed back inside, Iain fell to his knees in the corridor, crying and bargaining with God. If she survived this he swore, he would never again allow anyone to make their decisions for them. He would never again let her out of his sight. He would be a different man, a stronger man, a worthy husband, who protected her from charlatans like this surgeon. No-one had ever blamed himself quite as much as Iain did that fateful afternoon.

A few hours later they managed to save Susan's life, but the fight for survival was far from over. No-one knew what truly happened in that theatre and no-one could really understand it either. The tumour was larger and deeper than they had expected, her allergy to the steel instruments was unheard of and completely unexpected and her brain had suffered irreparable damage.

After years of further operations, Susan is still alive, but no-one really knows why. Both her legs have been amputated below the hips, she has a stoma bag in her stomach, and she will need to use a catheter for the rest of her life. Her muscular strength is so poor that she can't support herself in a wheelchair and she can barely speak. She is only seventy, but her quality of life is less than that of the deceased.

But Susan is still such a lovely human being. She braved the cards dealt to her by life and she carries the burden with a grace and kindness that I will never understand. She greets every visitor with a soft smile and she never complains.

The burden, however, is much harder for Iain to bear. The day after that operation he laid complaints against the hospital and the surgeon. For years he spent every waking moment either by Susan's bedside, supporting her in her fight to survive, or in the courts, fighting for his honour as her husband. He finally won both cases and as compensation the hospital paid out a lump sum. The surgeon received a warning and his practice was never the same after that. Iain used the money to install a special hospital bed for Susan. One that would turn her body every few minutes to prevent her from getting any bedsores. He converted their sunroom to a hospital room where she could enjoy the heat of the sun and the wave of the trees whenever she wanted to, and had a specialised system installed that not only controlled the heating and lights, but also measured the oxygen and carbon monoxide levels. He spent the last few hundred pounds on a landscape gardener who remodelled their little garden.

And since then he has spent every day of his life sitting in a corner of the room, watching her like a hawk. He has folders and folders filled with tables of information and care statistics. It is an absolute nightmare for us carers because we have to record every detail of our visit in triplicate on his forms. And then before we leave, he has to check all the information to confirm its accuracy and truth. He checks every single item we bring into or take out of the room. He allows no visitors out of fear of the germs they might carry in which could inevitably lead to Susan's death. She stares out over the garden, but she is not allowed the pleasure of a single plant in her room, just in case they carry a deadly disease or insect. Her one son phones often but never visits because he is not allowed to hug or even touch his own mum. The other son has broken all contact with them. Iain believes it is because they blame him for letting her down when he should have protected her. Susan knows that it is because they hate seeing her live the remainder of her years as a prisoner. But her love for him prevents her from ever telling him.

At the end of each visit I stand at my car and listen to the other carer complain about the husband being such a control freak and how he makes his own wife's life, and our lives, a living hell. And I can't help but wonder who the real prisoner is. Because Susan still lives. She still has love and soul left in her bones.

Yet, Iain's entire life is dependent on her existence. And his soul is long forgotten.

Pining for a Life that Once Was

One day I walked into Lady C's apartment. She was leaning over to the side and staring at something none of us could see. Her hair was a soft, silver-grey bob and her eyes were the saddest I have ever seen.

Talking to her was like listening to a waterfall of soft feathers. You had to practically hold your ear to her lips to hear anything she said and even then, it wasn't very clear. With each passing breath she desperately clung onto a life she no longer wanted to live, and I got the impression that breathing was the hardest job she has ever had to do.

She had two sons and a daughter, and they strived to give them the best life possible. Her husband had a good job and he was very proud of it, and as was common at the time, he spent the majority of his time at work and she spent her time at home, caring for their children. He lived to work but found pleasure in his beautiful wife and children and the home she had given him. They spaced the children out evenly, as was expected, which meant that their children had the best of everything. The best schools, the best activities, a house in the right area, friends of the right calibre, everything.

And then the children grew up and left home to make a new life for themselves. Her eldest moved to

Canada and has not returned in over thirty years. His children have never set foot on British soil and their accents are difficult to understand. But it was understandable. Sons leave their parents and cleave to their wives and children, and subsequently the wife's family. That is just how life works. It is just such a pity if the wife never really cares to meet or engage with his side of the family. But it is what it is. He found a woman he loved, and he had beautiful children and that was good enough for Lady C. She visited twice, once with her husband and once after his passing.

No-one expected him to die two years after his retirement.

Her second son married a beautiful English rose, and had a few years of happiness before he followed in his father's footsteps and threw himself into his work. It was a different era, a time when psychology told us that too much work is detrimental to a person and his family's mental health and the expectations on men especially were becoming remarkably different. And as is the case with change that happens too quickly, too many, including him, were not ready for it and so his marriage failed, and he missed the majority of his children's youth. Lady C could never really understand that. She blamed his wife for all of his shortcomings and her animosity cost her a lot of precious time with her grandchildren. Her daughter-in-law tried her absolute best, but there were only so many times she could reach out after being chased away.

Lady C's daughter was exactly as you would expect. A good wife to her husband, an excellent mother to her children and a good daughter to her parents. She involved them in all of their school activities and ensured that they spent the majority of their weekends and holidays together. She knew that her son-in-law was not very happy with the arrangement, but it worked so well. They were content to lose both their sons because that was the law of life, but that same law ensured that their daughter would be theirs forever. Perhaps it was the involvement and care of her daughter that made the sadness and longing for her sons so bearable. Acceptable even.

When her husband died it was her daughter who phoned the funeral director. She told her brothers and the rest of the family. She arranged the entire funeral and logistics and catered for everyone's needs, except the brother in Canada, because even his father's death could not get him to come home.

After the funeral it was also her daughter who sat down with her to prepare her for the future. They planned everything to the finest detail. She would sell her house and use the money to buy a small flat right next to the children's school. The rest of the money would be invested in a trust to ensure that she had enough money to pay for carers when the time came. She was adamant not to be a burden to her daughter. The plan was never for her to stay there forever. She would simply live there while the children were still at school, to make it easier for her daughter to drop by and for her to see her grandchildren regularly. When they had all grown up and flown the nest, she would move in with her daughter and her husband who would then take care of her until the end. That was the agreement. The flat was in an affluent area so it would rise in value, and when it was finally sold the money would be their inheritance. It was large enough for her to live comfortably, with a lounge, dining room, kitchen and two bedrooms, in case her son ever managed a visit.

Everything worked out as planned. She got the perfect flat, saw her daughter daily, her son once a week and received monthly telephone calls from Canada.

And then the unthinkable happened. The one thing that no-one saw coming. Lady C's beautiful daughter was diagnosed with a very aggressive form of cancer which erased all but her legacy in just a few short months.

Lady C's son from Canada could not manage a visit. Her other son had no idea what to do. Her daughter-in-law tried her best, but Lady C still wouldn't allow her to come too close. And for the first time in her life she realised just how lonely she truly was. She never had any friends, because her life was filled with that of her daughter. She never had a proper relationship with her sons because they never really wanted one and she never really needed them to. She met one set of grandchildren only twice, the other set tried their best, but they could never measure up to her daughter's children, her true favourites, and they knew it. As life would have it, her son-in-law moved to be nearer to his own parents and she now sees them only once every three months for a brief visit and she gets the occasional phone call as and when they remember.

The loss and reality of the situation was just too much for Lady C. She had a massive stroke a month after her daughter's passing, and although it caused no real damage, it broke her spirit. Or perhaps her spirit broke when her daughter breathed her last breath.

She couldn't walk because she didn't want to. She couldn't dress herself because she didn't want to. She couldn't function on her own anymore, because she didn't want to.

That is how we met. Her son wanted her to move to Canada, but she couldn't bear to be so far from her beloved grandchildren, and so she agreed that they use the trust fund to pay for a care package. She gets daily visits. Two in the morning, two in the afternoon and two at night. We wake her up, take her to the toilet, wash her, feed her and leave her to watch her daughter's favourite programmes on television. And at night we settle her in bed with a radio in one hand and a tissue in the other, to dry the tears that just keep coming.

Her son still visits every week. His ex-wife spends two nights a week to help her to the loo, not that she welcomes the help but she doesn't really have a choice. An overnight carer is just too expensive. And their children visit her every Sunday. She still gets monthly calls from Canada and quarterly visits from her most beloved. But her attention will always be with the one who isn't there anymore.

Before we take her to the toilet, she grabs her hairbrush as she remembers that her daughter always told her to brush her hair when she goes past a mirror. Back in the lounge we turn the television onto BBC Sport, one of her daughter's favourite channels. And at night, before we turn off the lights, we can hear her whisper: 'Goodnight, my child' before closing her eyes to try and drown the sorrow in sleep.

She takes four antidepressants a day. She struggles to sleep. She eats very little. She is barely still alive. She has lost everything that has made her life worth living, and yet the one thing she craves with her entire being, death, just won't come.

An Unimaginable Tragedy

Down by the docks, between the council houses and estates, I had the pleasure of spending three hours of my life.

Most appointments require a certain amount of personal care, and some cleaning or tidying but occasionally the visit is primarily to keep someone company. This was one of those situations.

The agency couldn't give me a lot of information apart from telling me that Morrie was a quadriplegic who needed round-the-clock care. My presence would enable his full-time carer a few hours respite to do her monthly shopping and errands.

With this tiny amount of information, I got into my car and drove to his house, allowing at least half an hour extra to read a few newspaper articles so that I would indeed have something to say. Without some general knowledge three hours could become quite a long time.

When I rang the bell, the door was opened by a jovial larger-than-life Amazon woman. She was born on an exotic island and she hadn't lost an ounce of her cultural identity in her ten years of living abroad. She wore a full-length, wide floral skirt, a yellow knit and a large red necklace and her shoulder-length hair seemed soft and glowing. She greeted me with a hearty laugh and told me not to look so worried, that Morrie was a darling and that I had no reason to feel uneasy. To be honest, up until that point I had no idea that I felt uneasy or worried, but I suppose next to her beauty I must have looked a little grey.

But I have never shied away from a challenge and so I pulled my shoulders back, took a deep breath and forced my heart to beat a little slower. I followed her to the kitchen where she introduced me to Morrie.

There at the table, with a brand-new Apple MacBook, was one of the most handsome men I have ever seen in my life. Except for my own husband and maybe even Johnny Depp, I have never seen his likeness. His face reminded me of the Greek gods and with pitch black hair and bright blue eyes it was impossible not to stare, but what really caught my eye was his height. Even in a wheelchair it was clear that this man was at least two metres tall and his presence filled the room with a gentle peace.

After brief introductions, the beauty left me standing there, unsure of whether to approach him or not. I remembered her promise that he doesn't bite, and I finally decided to venture a little closer. Of course, he just sat there, quietly waiting for me to take the first step. It had nearly annoyed me, until I remembered that he couldn't take that first step, even if he wanted to, and that he must have grown accustomed to waiting for other people to get over their awkwardness and approach him instead.

I was still trying to make sense of the situation when he asked me if I knew how to mix a Martini.

Gosh, I have never even poured myself a glass of wine and now this man wanted me to mix him such a sophisticated drink. 'Uhm, no sir, sorry. That is the one thing I can't do' I heard myself utter while I found a place for my bag.

'Don't worry about it. I will teach you' he promised. 'Do you see that bottle of gin? Pour a full cap into that silver flask. Add a little vermouth and then some ice cubes. Yes, that looks enough. Now you need to mix it well by shaking it as hard as you can. No, shake it a little more. Perfect. You will find a glass in the cabinet behind you. You see, I told you it won't be difficult.'

'Now, I know you are here to care for me, but I am actually busy writing my doctoral thesis and could really do with some silence. Your presence is not so much to keep me company as it is to ensure that my catheter bag doesn't get too full. If it isn't emptied in time my body can go into shock and I obviously can't do it myself. So, go sit in the lounge and make yourself comfortable, and just come to check on me every twenty minutes or so.'

And with that I left the kitchen and tried to find my way to the lounge. The flat was one of many in a group of high risers, and it was very dimly lit. 'You can turn on the lights' he called from the kitchen and I realised just how powerful his other senses must be, having lost his ability to move. With the click of the light I saw that the entire room was more like a library than a lounge. It took me nearly an hour and at least two catheter-checks before I finally settled on a book to read.

Another hour later his catheter bag was finally full and needed to be emptied. What a performance. I had to pull him to the centre of the kitchen, and even though I am stronger than I look, his height and weight were still a little too much for me and I finally understood why he needed an Amazon to look after him. Once in the centre of the room I had to go and get the bucket from the bathroom and open the little tap of the catheter to empty it into the bucket. I then had to flush it down the toilet before I could push him back to his original position. That was the only time I saw his bravado and charm make way for shame and sadness...

He asked me to cook some rice for supper, and whether it was his shame or my silence I'll never know, but that's when he decided to talk to me.

First, we discussed his age. Then how difficult it was for wheelchair users to get around the city. He explained that that is what his thesis was all about. He was an architect by trade, and he hated how inaccessible the city still was, even in today's day and age. 'Were you born this way?' I finally managed to ask the question that had plagued me all along and the look of surprise on his face made me feel incredibly bad for asking.

'Goodness, no! I was once a very strong and handsome young man. At least, that's what other people told me. I was a brilliant athlete and I had the world at my feet. After I finished my degree, I went to visit a friend in America. He had a beautiful house and invited all of us to come for a week's holiday. Upon arrival I wanted to show them just what an amazing swimmer I was and without checking I have dived into the shallow end of the pool. If I had only waited a few seconds they could have warned me. But I didn't and so I cracked my head, broke my back and caused irreparable damage. They had to fly me back to England and I spent nearly a year in hospital. I was in a coma at first, and then I had to live through the hell of awareness and understanding. No, don't feel sorry for me. It was just a mistake. One stupid mistake which changed the course of my life forever. What could I do about it? I wasn't dead, so I might as well try to live. Careful, I think the rice is going to burn!'

Years of experience and working with people could not prepare me for such a tragic story, that was told with such simplicity and matter-of-factness. I wanted to comfort him; I wanted him to know that I cared. But I had no idea what to say or do to move the conversation forward and in that silence the Amazon entered. She must have waited in the hallway until he had finished his story, and in a few minutes she had me gather my belongings, say my goodbyes, and walked me to the door. Outside she told me that Morrie enjoyed my company. 'How do you know' I wondered?

'It's simple, really. He doesn't tell his story to just anyone. He must have felt very safe with you.'

I got into my car, closed the door, and drove a few hundred yards until I was out of view, and then I allowed the tears to stream freely.

Survival

Some people become prisoners in their own bodies. Some are imprisoned by their own culture or faith. Some can't escape it, no matter how hard they try. Others don't want to escape it.

Petra was one of the loveliest people I have ever met. She was a young woman of thirty-five with the most aggressive form of Motor Neuron Disease I have ever seen. She was diagnosed at twenty-two and in just over ten years she had lost the use of most of her muscles. She could still just about use her tongue, but as soon as she lost that function, she wouldn't be able to swallow or talk anymore.

MND is the worst kind of illness. I always thought Alzheimer's was bad, but I now know it is only bad for those around you, as the sufferer has no idea what is really happening. MND on the other hand, robs you of everything that makes you you. Your muscles, your senses, your humanity, absolutely everything but your intellectual capacity. Which means you live a life in which you can't do anything for yourself; you are entirely dependent on other people and you KNOW it. You are aware just how big a burden you are becoming and there is no escape. And even though the quality of life is poor, people with MND tend to live a long life. I can't think of a more accurate impression of hell, no matter how hard I try.

Petra's life was even more complicated. You see she married her high school sweetheart at the age of twenty and she knew how proud it made her father. They planned to wait five years before starting a family because her husband had to first prove himself in his job, and she had to prove herself in his heart. Her beloved father died two years later and another two months after that her world came to a second, and this time, near complete halt.

The diagnosis was a bitter pill to swallow. The doctors were very clear about her life expectancy and the quality of life that lay ahead, and her husband, a boy of twenty-two, could not imagine a life with a severely handicapped wife. You must be thinking that he was the scum of the earth. Believe me, I did. But when I thought about it realistically, I understood just how hard it must have been for him as well. Although they only really liked each other, they got married young because their parents approved of the match. He expected to grow in his love for her, as they made a life together and started a family, but they were only young and practically still strangers after a few short years. Some men would turn to other women. In fact some do, without the excuse of such a horrible diagnosis. Some women would as well. At the very least, they would ask for a divorce. Petra's husband wasn't an exception to the rule. In fact, he was just an ordinary young man.

What made his situation exceptional was their culture's aversion to divorce. It just wasn't done. And even though he tried to argue his way out of it, Petra just wouldn't agree. Her devotion to both her culture and her father kept them bound for the rest of their lives.

And so I walked into one of the saddest situations I have ever experienced. Petra's house, like any other, had two doors. Her husband used the back door and her family and carers used the front. They had two bedrooms in the house, one for her and one for him. The two rooms were right next to each other and they shared a kitchen, lounge, corridor, and bathroom but they agreed to never acknowledge each other again. So he would wake up, have a shower, make himself breakfast and watch television without looking in her direction. I once walked past him in the hallway, and I was shocked to be treated as if I were completely invisible. And she hadn't mentioned his name in years. As if he didn't exist. Her family paid her share of the mortgage and bills, and he paid the rest. On paper they had a very happy life. In reality, it was the life of two ghosts.

There was nothing wrong with Petra's intellect. She couldn't hold a glass of water on her own, but she could tell you a joke that would make you cry with laughter. She couldn't get out of bed by herself, but she could make you cry with tales of her childhood. She was slowly losing her speech, but she still managed to pray to her god and her father every night. The light in her eyes hadn't been dimmed yet.

There were times when I felt so sorry for them both. I couldn't imagine such a loveless life. A shared life where you pretend not to notice the existence of another. How do you live such a life? How do you cope with such a dreaded illness, knowing that the one person who swore to stand by you couldn't even bear to look at you anymore?

Other times I was so incredibly angry with them both. When we put her to bed at night, we had to attach an alarm to her cheek so that she could attempt to set it off by pushing her head against the pillow when she couldn't breathe or when her legs got caught in her blankets. The alarm sounded out loud enough for the community to hear, to alert the community support service of her situation, but her own husband, who slept right next door to her, ignored it completely How?

How?

There were times when I heard him cry alone in his room. It was such a loud, sad cry of hopelessness and sorrow, a testament to a life of loneliness. I think the workhouse howl must have sounded similar. And all the while she continued to watch television and pretended not to hear. How?

How?

And then, time and again, when I walked into her house and saw her smile and looked into her sparkling eyes I knew that there was nothing quite as strong as a human being. We would always find a way to survive. Even if it was a helpless, speechless, loveless life. We would always find a way to survive.

Because mere survival is still much better than the alternative.

Acknowledgments

First and foremost I want to say a massive thank you to my mother in law, Linda Majcher and my sister, Nadia Lamprecht, for their help in editing and proofreading this translation. I could not have done it without their expertise and support.

Thank you Anni Buchner for designing the cover art for both the Afrikaans and English versions of this book. Your work is stunning and I am proud to use it! Thank you also Drikus and Anni for your love and support these last two years.

Thank you also to my publishers, Malherbe Uitgewers, and in particular Heleen Malherbe, for being willing to publish this translation alongside the Afrikaans version.

Thank you mamma (Mariaan) for encouraging me to submit my very first manuscript and to translate it. Most of all, thank you for your continuous love, support, and encouragement.

Pappa, I love you and miss you every day. Thank you for always believing I could do it. It was your text about my first published book that kept me going until it was finally a reality.

Iain, Andrew, Maria, Lily, Richard and William- thank you for loving me unconditionally, even when I am grumpy and annoyed when the words don't flow as I want them to.

And finally, thank you to my Heavenly Father for blessing me with this life. I am nothing without You and I am so incredibly privileged to know and serve You in everything I do.